Falling Apart

Stephanie Anne

Published by Stephanie Anne, 2023.

FALLING APART

First edition. November 21, 2023.

ISBN: 979-8223155935

Written by Stephanie Anne.

Table of Contents

To my wonderful husband Mark who keeps me from falling apart

The Wearisome Dead: My Hatred of Zombies

W*arning: The following contains spoilers of some of my previously published works*

• • • •

Maybe hate is a strong word, but the version of Stephanie in her early 20s severely disliked zombies. Back in those days, the only horror fiction I read was by Thomas Harris and Stephen King. The only horror movies I could handle were popular classics from the 70s and 80s as I was too scared to tackle anything modern. All I knew about zombies was what pop culture and Scooby Doo taught me throughout my childhood and teenage years. I thought they were far less interesting than vampires, werewolves, and ghosts. Boring, even.

What's funny is one of my first horror movie experiences involved the undead: John Carpenter's *The Fog* (1980). As I understood it, this was a ghost story. Over half a lifetime later, I would now argue this is about zombies risen from their watery grave. Whatever they may or may not be, the important part is that I enjoyed the film.

I remember my mom telling me she and my dad went to see *The Fog* in theatres for date night. Afterwards, they were both freaked out whenever the shower filled with steam. For 14-year-old me watching it in the early 2000s I expected to be terrified, but the dated special effects saved me. Whether the film is about ghosts or zombies, this is still one of my favourite horror movies.

In those early years of my horror education, I preferred zombies when I could rationalize them as something else. If the undead had a clear purpose and / or spoke coherently, I enjoyed their presence. However, if they shambled aimlessly, doing nothing but growl and bite, they were plain, boring zombies. I could ignore that Frank from *Hellraiser* (1987) is close to being a zombie because he is smart and seductive. His status as a member of the undead is questionable, though. Did he die, or simply exist on a different plane of reality before coming back to our own?

Then there's *The Evil Dead* (1981). Sure, they come back to "life" to torment the living, but those re-animated corpses can't possibly be zombies because what they are is in the title. Looking back, that logic is flimsy at best. Speaking of re-animation, 1985's *Re-Animator* doesn't have zombies, just re-animated corpses. At least, that's what I told myself. But what is a re-animated corpse if not a zombie? I am astounded at the mental gymnastics I've done in the past to distance myself from the thought I might actually enjoy zombie movies.

And don't even get me started on the undead / zombies in the cult classic *Plan 9 from Outer Space* (1959). No, seriously. Do not get me started. One of the beefier papers I wrote for my MA was about Ed Wood and his films. I have *a lot* to say about that movie but we don't have that kind of space in this book.

All of these instances in horror films bring to mind an interesting question. What is the distinction between zombies and the undead? In many of the movies I've mentioned so far, the creatures blur the line and the argument could be made for either classification. It doesn't stop there. Are Frankenstein's monster or mummies considered zombies? My husband and

I heavily debated this topic and have yet to come to an agreement. The term "undead" can also refer to other classic horror creatures like vampires or any kind of revenant monster. So, all zombies are undead, but not all undead are zombies. Where is the line drawn?

In *The Element Encyclopedia of Magical Creatures* by John and Caitlin Matthews, almost the entire entry under the letter Z is devoted to zombies. "[...] A dead human being whose own soul is absent but whose body can be inspirited by the will to work." I'll spare you the whole three-page entry. The key points involve an examination of the history and making of traditional zombies, ending with a brief description of their presence in film. They are described as "robotic [...], torn from the grave." Not a thrilling way to spend the afterlife.

Maybe that's why the concept of undead is preferable to zombie for me. An undead creature like a vampire, the Headless Horseman, or even Frank from *Hellraiser*, comes with power. You are (un) dead but you gain something in the process: physical strength, supernatural abilities, or knowledge. Despite moments of weakness and vulnerability, there's little suggestion of helplessness. You're a formidable monster that can scheme and plan to defeat the heroes of the story. Whether the monster succeeds or not is another matter.

By comparison, zombies are associated with negative connotations. *The Element Encyclopedia* speaks of zombies as having no soul, but whose body can work. Think about zombies in *Night of the Living Dead* (1968) or in *28 Days Later* (2002). The Living Dead are mindless corpses who wander aimlessly looking for their next meal. They haven't gained anything from their new condition. In more modern films like

28 Days, the zombies are associated with illness and infection: loss of agency, loss of health, loss of life. Then again, some vampire stories have treated the affliction like a disease. Again, another blurred line.

In fact, one of my early zombies walks her own blurred line. When I wrote "Kacie", I pictured her as a ghoulish entity like something out of *The Grudge* (2004). (I'm referencing the American remake here specifically because of my long and complicated history with the film.) However, when I look back at my description of Kacie in the climactic moment, she could easily be a zombie. We never learn *how* she comes back into her father's life. She just appears. We don't know if she's a soul struggling to move on, or a recently revived corpse. I'm still not certain if Kacie will ever tell me if she is a zombie or a ghost. Or something else entirely.

So, can I even say I hate zombies as a whole? Or do I hate one specific version of zombies and it's taken me almost 10 years to realize it?

Google "zombie movies" and most of the top titles that come up are films I have seen. And yes, I enjoyed a number of them and would re-watch them if I haven't already. If you Google "zombie books", I haven't read as many of the titles but I do have some of them shelved as "want to read" on Goodreads. Experience has taught me that if someone recommends a specific zombie book I will read it without question.

Two zombie books that stand out are *World War Z* by Max Brooks and *The Girl with All the Gifts* by M. R. Carey. Both two different versions of zombies, although both are born from disease and illness. The zombies in *World War Z* are the kind of shambling, mindless drones I'm not a fan of. I did enjoy certain parts of the book, but as a whole I found it underwhelming. I did not enjoy the film, but mostly because it lacked the epistolary and episodic structure of the book. I'm a sucker for epistolary stories.

By comparison, I fell in love with *The Girl with All the Gifts*. Before I was even aware of the book's existence, I watched the 2016 movie with Mark during our first year together. One of our date nights involved pizza delivery and a zombie movie with a premise interesting enough to intrigue my horror intolerant partner. I loved it so much I immediately went out and bought the book. Yes, you guessed it, I loved the titular character because she's an intelligent and empathetic zombie as opposed to a mindless sack of flesh. I think it's safe to say we're noticing a trend.

And then, there's my most recent "zombie" read. An argument I've come across repeatedly is that horror fiction reflects the real horrors of the time. In W. Scott Poole's *Wasteland: The Great War and the Origins of Modern Horror,* he analyzes the ways the war impacted multiple aspects of art and literature. I've heard the stories of my shell-shocked great-grandfather, and how fighting in the trenches affected him. But it wasn't until I listened to a certain passage in the audiobook that I stopped to consider the zombies that came home after fighting in the war.

These hollowed out men, some physically disfigured, would have been very real and horrific representations of undead monsters. Again, this is a zombie created by loss, and the nature of said loss makes their existence all the more painful and uncomfortable. I've since come to the conclusion that it might be beneficial for me to seek out more horror stories and movies from the years immediately following The Great War. I'm sure will it further change my perspective on these horror monsters.

I think I also have an increased love of the horror genre as a whole to thank for my slowly growing appreciation for zombies. I didn't always used to be such a hardcore horror fan – and I didn't think I'd ever become a horror author. Much like the creation of this collection, the genre crept up on me. Now I'm watching and reading so much more horror than before, opening my mind to new scary and gruesome experiences. I've become more familiar with the different types and sub-categories of monsters. An increased understanding of zombies allowed me to love some of them. Not all. Some.

Although I haven't always been a fan of horror, I have loved science fiction from an early age. So, of course, some of my favourite horror tropes and stories are the ones that blend my love of the two genres. Since zombies in post-apocalyptic fiction can be explained into existence by science, it's astounding to me that zombies aren't my favourite monster. Depending on the nature of their creation and the particulars of the story they inhabit, these horrific creatures can start to cross over into the realm of sci-fi.

The apocalypse is how zombies ended up in my writing in the first place. Yes, I am referring to the chaos of 2020. Losing my job at the start of the pandemic provided me with the opportunity to get started on my publishing career, while allowing me more time to write and explore different styles and genres. From this hellscape of uncertainty and experimentation "Hank's Cabin" was born.

Originally written for a ReedsyPrompts, I used the prompt to experiment with a subtle zombie story. Hank is preparing himself for something, but the reader doesn't know it's the zombie apocalypse until the end. I like to write stories where you don't get the full reveal until the finale. It doesn't have to be a twist ending, per se, but a reveal nonetheless. It's because any situation is much more frightening if you don't know what the danger is. Things get scarier when your imagination fills in the blanks.

That's another way I like my zombies – a mystery until the end. I employed a similar trick in "Cold Cuts & Cigarettes". The story was inspired by the AutoCrit 2022 Community Writing Challenge where the prompt was, well, community. It just so happened that my uncle's funeral took place around the same time the challenge began. So, with death on the brain, it was inevitable that this story of a close-knit community should also be about zombies.

Uncle Bob is a zombie I fell in love with. Based on my own Uncle Rob, who lived a strange, sad, and chaotic life, Bob is largely absent from the bulk of the story. Yet his presence represents all of the fears and insecurities of the narrator. He is arguably the most important character, and I hope I was able to do him justice.

Now more zombies have started to infiltrate my writing. Two more AutoCrit challenges provided inspiration and prompts that helped birth hellish post-apocalyptic landscapes. Inevitably, those apocalypses bred zombies. Not the stereotypical, mindless, shambling kind; my own unique versions of the undead and near-dead. And a third challenge led me to create a revenant from the grave, clawing her way out of the earth and into the hapless narrator's life.

Talk about growth. Here I went from hating zombies in my 20s to writing about zombies in my early 30s. I guess people can change. But wait, there's more! Two of my tattoos reference horror movies featuring zombies: *The Evil Dead* and *Re-Animator*. 22-year-old me would be shocked.

32-year-old me is proud to present this short story collection dedicated to zombies. Some of them are clear-cut, un-deniable, re-animated corpses, while others blur those pesky lines. I have living zombies, and dead zombies. Eloquent zombies, and growling zombies. A collage of undead on my own terms.

So, as you start this collection, I have to ask: do you like zombies? What kind?

Dentist

The phone would not stop ringing.

"Isn't anyone going to get that?" Charles shouted into the empty waiting room. The phone continued to ring.

Had it not been for the faint "I'll be with you shortly" he heard from the back room when he came in, he would have left by now.

"Ridiculous," he muttered.

There were plenty of lazy folks looking for reasons not to go into work, but he had not expected his dentist's office to be one of the businesses suffering from the labour shortage.

The TV, tuned to a local station at its lowest volume, droned on about the ongoing pandemic and how experts advised not to leave home unless necessary. Charles scoffed. Fake news. Another excuse for people to stay home from work and for Big Pharma to push more pills. *He* had certainly never seen an infected person.

Checking the time, Charles huffed. The dentist was now eight minutes late for the appointment. Unacceptable.

But before his watch reached the nine-minute mark, the same voice from before called out.

"I'm ready for you now. Come on back."

"It's about time," Charles said loud enough that had anyone else been in the waiting room, they could have heard. Yet not so loud that the dentist would hear.

After twenty years of visits—twenty years of cavities, root canals, and annual checkups—Charles knew where to go. Perhaps it was for the best the receptionist didn't come in today. Did his hard-earned money need to be paying the salary of someone who only had to show him which room to go in? Then the phone started up again, its shrill, tuneless tone echoing through the room, and he changed his mind.

When he entered the exam room, the dentist kept his back to the door as he set up his tools. Charles winced as something metal fell to the floor with an ear-splitting clang. He sat ungracefully in the plastic covered chair and waited.

"Be with you in a second," said the dentist, his voice hoarse and unfamiliar. Charles nodded, forgetting they had their backs to each other in the tiny room.

"Alrighty then," the dentist announced with a flourish as he slid his rolling stool across the floor to Charles' side. "What brings you in today, Mr. Carns?"

"Well, as I told your *incompetent* receptionist—who, by the way, I noticed is absent this morning, very unprofessional—my upper left molar is—"

Charles stared into the grey, drooping eyes of the man beside him. The skin surrounding the eyes was also grey; it looked as if the surgical mask he wore over the lower half of his face was the only thing keeping everything from sloughing off.

"You're not my usual dentist."

"No," said the man as he removed his mask. Beneath was a lipless mouth and bloody teeth, chunks of flesh still stuck between them. "I'm new."

Charles didn't have a chance to voice his complaint. The teeth sank into his throat and tore out his larynx.

Hank's Cabin

I t may not have been the best choice, but at least it had been a choice. Few people had that luxury these days.

Hank stood by the window, looking out at the freshly fallen snow, feeling only a mild chill in his old bones. Normally, the cabin looked out over onto the lake, but today the lake was buried. The only colour that stood out against the white landscape and grey sky was the hint of dark evergreen trees on either side of the lake. They, too, were blanketed with snow.

"Wish you were here with me, Lacey."

Hank sighed, and his breath fogged up the glass. Quickly, and almost without thinking about it, he wiped the fog away with the sleeve of his shirt. He noticed that the edges of his sleeve were frayed. With a shrug, he left himself a mental note to search for his late wife's sewing kit if he had the time. He wasn't good enough with a needle and thread to fix the problem, but he could at least tidy it up with a pair of scissors.

"Scissors. Yes. Those'll come in handy."

He moved his mental note up further in the queue. He wouldn't mind having a pair of scissors in case of an emergency. And he was certain he'd be seeing his fair share of emergencies.

But the first thing on his mental list was to take stock of what he had in the pantry. There was no electricity at the cabin – Hank had never seen the point – so there was no fridge, but there was always something leftover in the pantry from the last trip up to the lake. This time, Hank was not disappointed. There were quite a few canned goods carefully lined up, labels out, on the wooden shelves. More than he remembered, actually. His son always loved to point out that Hank's memory seemed to be deteriorating. Hank usually begged to differ.

"You might just be on to something this time, Justin."

With a shrug, Hank walked across the tiny cabin to the front hall where his bags lay. He picked up the largest duffle bag and dragged it into the kitchen. It was filled with all of the food items he had brought from home. He didn't want to leave anything behind. It would have been a waste if all the food at home went bad while he was up at the cabin. He even brought the contents of his fridge. Some of the more perishable items would have to be eaten right away, but Hank was confident that he could set something up with all that snow to keep the rest of it fresh. He was pretty sure he had an old metal bucket lying around that would make the perfect makeshift mini-fridge if it was packed with enough snow.

Until the bucket was found, however, it was time for the next item on the mental list. Hank opened up each of his bags, putting everything away. Everything, even items he brought from home, always had specific spots within the small cabin. No matter what the rest of his life was like right now, he wasn't about to let this cabin turn into a dumping ground. No. Everything had its place. He could almost hear his wife chuckling in the corner, telling Hank that he was a silly old man.

"You can laugh all you want, Lacey. A little bit or organization never killed nobody. And you know damn well it's going to help me out a whole lot to know *exactly* where everything is when the scrambling starts."

As he went about putting his things away, Hank thoroughly inspected every room, making sure that there was nothing in need of repair. This was his usual ritual, but today it was especially important. If there were any spots in the cabin that looked like they needed special attention, Hank lifted his palm to feel for any cold air that might be trickling in from the outside. He marked the problem areas with pieces of green painter's tape. Just from looking outside, he could tell that it wasn't done snowing out there. The cabin would have to be thoroughly winterproofed, among other things.

During his inspection, he found both the bucket and the scissors, and he was quite pleased with himself. After trimming the edge of his sleeves and sticking the scissors in his pocket for safe keeping, he darted out the front door to fill the bucket with snow before scurrying back inside, keeping his head on a swivel. He closed the door gently, quietly, but locked it with vigour.

The metal sides of the bucket were so cold that he nearly dropped it before making it to the kitchen. And he shook the cold out of his fingers once it was safely on the ground. Hank tucked the bucket into a corner of the kitchen, away from the windows and as far away as possible from any potential sources of heat, before filling it with perishable goods.

He took a moment to admire his ingenuity before filling the pantry with non-perishables from the duffel bag.

There was plenty of food. More than enough to last a year. Or maybe longer. He certainly didn't want to have to go all the way into town for food if he could help it, especially with all of this snow. And he didn't have any neighbours close by to lend him anything, not that anyone was in a lending mood these days. No, Hank needed to make this food last as long as possible so that he could avoid going into town for as long as possible. Besides, he had no intention of going outside at all unless it was an emergency.

"Better start setting up traps for the squirrels too," he muttered to himself as he closed the pantry door. Squirrels were fatter this time of year, and he could probably get two to three meals out of one of them.

Once most of the tasks on his mental list were done, and Hank was starting to drag his feet, he decided to treat himself to a beer as he sat down in front of the fire. That had been the first task, of course. Once he dropped his bags at the front entrance, he immediately started on the fire. By now, it was roaring beautifully, dancing in the fireplace, and the cabin was deliciously warm.

Hank opened the beer but barely even took a sip before he was up off the couch again. His knees groaned in protest, but he paid them no mind. He made his way over to a locked cabinet and opened it with the keys that hung around his neck. Then, he pulled his shotgun out of the cabinet and brought it over to the couch. As he sat by the fire, letting the warmth seep into his bones, he cleaned his shotgun and sipped at his beer. This would have been a perfect way to spend the afternoon had the circumstances been different.

While his hands were busy with the shotgun, his mind became preoccupied with other things. He thought about his son, Justin. He couldn't remember the last time they had spoken. Maybe it had been a few weeks? Or maybe even longer? Well, it had at least been before it all went to hell, that was for sure. Hank thought about calling Justin once he reached the cabin, but eventually he decided against it. There had never been much cell service up by the lake, so there certainly wouldn't be any now. Justin probably wouldn't even have cell service in the city. Besides, Hank wasn't sure that anyone would even answer if he tried calling. As much as he hated to admit it, it was probably best to forget about ever seeing Justin again.

"I sure hope you're all right, boy."

With his shotgun cleaned and resting on the coffee table, Hank sat back and finished his beer as he looked out the window onto the lake. He loved that view, and it saddened him that this was probably the last time he was ever going to see it or be able to enjoy it. He wiped away a single tear with this sleeve before gulping down the remains of his beer.

Before getting up, he let his eyes drift from the window to the pile of lumber waiting by the door where his bags had been. After his brief rest on the couch, the next item on his mental list was to board up all the windows. After all, he thought sadly as he glanced down at his shotgun, it wouldn't be long until the undead started showing up.

Asleep at the Wheel

This was her fifth day on the road, traveling from one client meeting to the next. Her work-life consisted of waking up in a different town each morning, greasy takeout when she had the chance, and too many hours behind the wheel.

In order to save her precious per diem for a more substantial meal than an overcooked burger, she chose to sleep only at the cheapest motels. The consequence of her decision meant that even after three gritty and unsatisfying coffees, she was still in danger of letting her eyes close for longer than a blink.

Maybe if her tightwad of a boss would loosen the company purse strings a little when it came to business trips, so many of her colleagues wouldn't be quiet quitting. Maybe then she wouldn't be so overworked as she took on more and more and more of other people's clients. Maybe—

THWACK!

"Oh fuck!"

The car came to a screeching halt.

"Please let that be a deer."

Of course it wasn't.

Still tangled in her seatbelt, she toppled out of the open car door and staggered towards the body behind her bumper. Muddy tire tracks decorated the man's shirt. The snow around him turned red.

"Oh fuck, fuck, fuck. Hey mister? Mister, you okay? Oh God, please tell me you're okay. I'm gonna call…"

She gagged when she noticed his crushed ribcage.

"Oh God, I'm gonna lose my job, I'm gonna go to jail..."

This time, her gag had substance, and she spit a mouthful of bile into the snow at her feet.

"Oh fuck, I gotta call an ambulance. I'm gonna call you an ambulance. Just please, *please*, don't be dead."

While she wrestled her phone out of her pocket, she thought she saw movement out of the corner of the eye. Holding her breath, she looked back at the body on the road. The man stirred. She almost collapsed with relief.

"Oh you're—"

Despite a misshapen torso, he was on his hands and knees, breathing so hard she could hear it over her own heartbeat.

"Thank God you're okay. Well, you're not okay, but you're... I am so, so sorry. My company will pay for—I mean, I'm not sure if they'll..."

She couldn't believe it. He was on his feet.

"B-but I'll pay anything they don't. I... You don't know how happy I am to...to..."

He was facing her now, staring at her with milky eyes and an open mouth. Drool trickled over his drooping lips. Tendrils of saliva swayed in the breeze. His skin was pockmarked with frostbite and gangrene.

"S-sir? I think you need to go to a hospital."

He didn't share with her his opinion on the matter. Before she had a chance to scream, he buried his teeth in her throat.

The Stranger Across the Bar

L ook to the left. To the right. No one around. Sprint across the road, keep your knees bent to a crouch. There might be someone watching from the windows above. There might not be. Either way, no one will see you. This isn't your first supply run. You know how to avoid being seen. And how to avoid being caught.

Your back slams into the wall as you throw yourself up against the building. Not hard enough to knock the breath out of you, or to make a sound, but hard enough you'll end up with bruises. Not the worst thing that could happen.

Pause.

Eyes to the left and the right. Safe to proceed. Keep your head on a swivel.

Inching towards the door of the dilapidated bar, the broken glass on the sidewalk indicates that someone broke in once before, maybe at the beginning of the first wave. The shards of glass are caked in grime. There likely won't be much left. But people were choosy about their supplies back then. Water, first aid kits, your child's favourite food. They didn't always get what they wanted. When you're forced to hurry, things get missed. During the second wave, a supply run was for anything that might be left over. Grocery stores, mega marts, convenience stores all got picked clean. Abandoned restaurants were the next to get hit once civilization fell.

By the third wave onward, you're looking for anything that might have been left on purpose. Expired. Broken packaging. Mysterious substances that were once food and now a breeding ground for mould and maggots. All the things no one in their right mind would touch. However, with enough desperation, a person can choke down even the most rancid meal found on the floor. Any insects that have taken root in your meal are just extra protein.

Food is the new commodity. Money lost all value early on. It was starvation that led to the fall of, well, everything. The first wave was ash, rained down from the sky after being belched up by a long dormant volcano in British Columbia. It brought harsh weather and drought on a global scale, killing crops and livestock with painful slowness. Despite record profits for years before, the major grocery chains hiked the prices yet again. Supply and demand. Theft was the new normal. Fights broke out in grocery stores. The impoverished were the first to die.

The second wave brought the infection. You're not entirely sure how it happened because you and many others had already lost power. News was, and is, rare and infrequent. Someone ate something they shouldn't. A toxic plant. Maybe contaminated human waste. Could've even been a rabid animal. Starvation drove patient zero to unleash the unthinkable. The sickness spread fast. It crossed continents on the wind, like a cancerous pollen. It decimated cities as it passed via bodily fluids, constantly changing and evolving. Not even the best scientists could keep up with the new strains.

By the time the third wave hit... Well, the severely infected have now found a new source of food, making them that much more dangerous. The rest of us are still hunting for scraps.

With an iron pipe raised like it's the bottom of the ninth and you're ready to hit a home run, you shimmy into the dark bar through the remains of the door. The air is thick with mould and mildew. Stifling a cough in the back of your throat, you make your way to the counter.

The shelves on the formerly mirrored wall have all been picked clean of all the best liquors. Only the dregs and sugar crystals remain in bottles no one was desperate enough to want, now displayed in front of a cracked wall with chipped paint and shards of mirror.

The doors of the mini fridges below the countertop bump your shins. The last person to scavenge here didn't bother to close them. They're all empty, save for a long-since expired jar of cocktail onions. You decide to try your luck. There are worse ways to die than food poisoning. And your stomach is aching.

They're sour and rancid, burning your tongue, and you plug your nose to choke down as many as possible. Your body takes over when it realizes you're feeding it, and you practically swallow the onions whole. You would drink the brine too if it wasn't cloudy with mould. But you are tempted. Instead, you wash this scavenged meal down with Crème de Menthe that makes your eyes water. It's gritty on your tongue.

Churning in your gut warns you that this was not the best meal. You may pay for it later. For now, you've been fed. There's little pain, and you're prepared to face the consequences when they come. It won't be the first time you've had to hole up in a safe, dark space and let the sickness pass.

After another regrettable swig from the bottle, you catch sight of it in a fragment of mirror. A reflection. A person. No, worse. The bottle shatters on the ground as your hand releases it to grab the iron pipe.

"Back off!" you shout at the figure in the doorway of the adjacent room as you swivel to face them.

They freeze, but an odd smile creeps to their chapped lips. Drooping eyelids cover cloudy eyes that still manage to see, despite the odds.

"Don't come any closer!"

They say nothing. They just keep smiling, revealing more and more yellowed teeth. Row after row, like a shark, all crowded on top of one another. Far too many teeth for a human mouth to hold.

"Are you sick?" You say it more like a command than a question, but your voice trembles. You already know the answer. Your eyes are darting back and forth, trying to plan a safe exit. You can't let them catch you.

"Aren't we all?" they say after a painfully long silence. "Sick of being forced to live like this? Starving, scared, and jumping at shadows. Aren't you sick?"

They take a step towards you and you drop the metal pipe. The clanging still echoes through the bar after you retrieve the revolver from your pocket. You said you would only use this in an emergency.

"Don't move! You're one of them, aren't you?"

The stranger smirks. "One of the monsters you mean?"

"One of the infected! Now stay back!"

They raise their hands in mock compliance. "Alright. If you insist."

"How long have you been sick?" You don't want to, but you need to figure out your odds for survival. If they're too far gone... Well, at least there's no one left to mourn for you.

The stranger smiles wider and their chapped lips stretch almost as wide as their scaly face. Blood dribbles into their mouth and onto their teeth. It mixes with mucous-like saliva that drips down one side of their chin. You stifle a gag and your breath tastes like rotten onions and mint.

"How long?" you repeat slowly.

"You should know exactly how long."

Your grip on the gun falters, but you readjust and try to steady your trembling hands.

"What do you mean?"

"Why, I'm you."

"No, you're not," you scoff. "Liar. You're shedding and I'm not." Your voice lacks confidence. You never actually looked at yourself in the broken mirror behind the bar. You were too focused on food.

The stranger carefully peels a strip of old, dried flesh off the back of one arm. They place it on their tongue as if it's a piece of wafer paper. They swallow without chewing.

"The sickness is making you crazy," you continue, as if somehow it helps. "Once the disease runs its course, your brain will be eaten away and you'll turn into a... a monster."

"At least we'll be well fed." They lick their lips with a thick, purple tongue. The onions in your stomach threaten to evacuate your body.

"I should put you out of your misery right now before things get bad. You'll thank me for it." No matter how hard you tense your aching fingers, you can't make them pull the trigger.

A barking laugh fills your ears. "*Your* brain is being eaten away. That's why you see me now. The hallucinations are starting. Pretty soon, a jar of onions won't be enough. You'll need *meat*."

"Stop with the games. It won't work." Your grip on the gun worries you.

Their smile widens past what you thought was physically possible.

"How many square feet do you think this bar is?"

"What?"

"Well, you appear to think this bar is sizeable enough to have an extra room attached."

"I... don't understand."

"This isn't a doorway I'm standing in. This is another mirror."

"No." But your voice is shaking, and the tremor returns to your hands.

Your eyes scan the edges of the... whatever it is that frames them, but it all blurs together. When was the last time you got any sleep? And you're so deliriously hungry. You can't see or think clearly. Still, it has to be a doorway. The person doesn't even look like you. But that's what the disease can do to your body.

No. You've heard the stories. The wild tales told at the trading posts. The infected will say anything to prolong their miserable lives. They're deceptively eloquent, but it's just the infection piloting the brain. There's nothing human left in them. Never believe a word they say. Never.

You release one hand from the gun to wipe the sweat off your brow with one grimy shirt sleeve and shiver.

"You have a fever," the stranger says. "You're infected."

"It's food poisoning," you grunt, thinking once more about the questionable meal you ate and swallowing bile. Your voice waivers all the same.

"Still, better safe than sorry. Aim the gun at your head."

The room spins and your knees buckle.

"What?"

"Well, if you're going to kill me, you should kill yourself too. After all, we are one person."

"We are not!"

"Then let me go free. Let us both go free."

Your finger twitches on the trigger.

"How about I just kill you instead?" You don't sound confident. Your head is pounding and the gun is heavy.

"Kill me and you die too. Do you really want to take that chance?"

"Yes. No. I..."

Rules for Not Dying
By P.J. Basford

1. When you meet a stranger on the road, ask them what the picture is on their phone's lock screen. If it is a normal person, they will tell you all about their kids, pets, significant other, or some little thing they enjoyed before the fall of civilization. If it is a nutcase, they might go on about how that's a stupid question to ask, how the government is spying on us through our phones, and they might even wave a gun around to prove their point. If it is a member of the undead, their answer will be garbled and unintelligent.

2. If the stranger is one of the nutcases, it is advisable that you change course and avoid confrontation. No matter how weak they may appear, the crazies will hand your ass to you nine times out of ten.

3. If the stranger is a zombie, kill immediately and burn the body.

4. If you have proven that this is a harmless, normal person very much attached to the subject of their phone screen, kill immediately. These kinds of people will not put up much of a fight and will likely be carrying a bit of extra fat on their bodies. Remember: fat equals flavour.

5. When resorting to cannibalism in order to keep yourself alive, be sure to cook your meat thoroughly. If any kind of thermometer or measuring device is

available to you, aim for an internal temperature of around 145 degrees Fahrenheit, or 63 degrees Celsius. (This is a rough conversion only.)

6. It is best to let the meat rest for five minutes before cutting into it. If you are able to forage some non-toxic mushrooms, those pair well with human flesh. It would be much nicer with a slice of fresh bread and some dipping sauce, but we have to make do with what we have.

7. Should you come across a corpse—fresh or otherwise—do not eat it. Unless you have made the kill yourself, there is no way to determine if the body belonged to one of the infected or not.

8. It is only safe to consume non-infected humans. Consuming the meat of an undead person will turn you into a brain-hungry, people-eating monster that shambles around with no intelligence or free will. Although that is technically not dying, it is a fate akin to death for the purposes of this rule book.

Domino Effect

"**S**tony, stony, dominoes," Me hummed, reaching its fingers deep into the soft ground and pulling up a handful of dominoes and mud. A strip of loose flesh peeled off its hand, sticking behind and almost melting into the earth. It didn't notice the pain anymore. Everything was pain.

Years of physical torment dulled the sensations that once drove this shell of a human past both their physical and mental breaking point. Exposed nerves and injuries that would never heal reduced it to no more than a nameless sack of meat. It was a miracle the flesh and bones still held together, but years of trial and error taught Me how to survive this soggy wasteland. Though it now wondered with increasing frequency if perhaps survival was worse than the inevitable.

One of the dominoes was missing, and Me checked the bag again to make sure it wasn't stuck to the inside again. It wasn't there. After a moment of puzzlement, Me remembered breaking it in frustration during the last game, throwing it against a barely standing cement wall. Both wall and domino shattered. That day Me was hoping to lose, but Me never lost a game of dominoes.

Although it's remaining globous and lidless eye was obscured by cataracts, Me imagined the remaining pieces were still as beautiful as the first day it found them. Despite the fading paint in the dot-like divots, and rough edges that showed signs of acid damage, they were still useable. Not many things could make that claim these days.

Adhering to rules only it knew of, Me laid out the dominoes in loose patterns across the ground, humming a non-existent tune. Thunder echoed across the darkening sky, but Me paid no mind. There was always rain. Even when the rain stopped, the thunder continued. And like all the rest stops before, nothing about this abandoned zoo would offer protection from the showers. Nowhere was safe, and getting wet was inevitable. Dryness was a concept long forgotten.

"What to do, to do today? Walk some more or pass away?" Me sang as it changed the configuration of the dominoes. Opaque drool leaked out of a gash in its lip. Me licked it away and spat out a malformed tooth.

The game wasn't the same without the missing piece and Me contemplated changing the rules, as it often did. Looking up from the game, one cloudy eye and one empty socket surveyed the enclosure.

"Bones, bones, give me some bones."

The rain had destroyed any remaining hints of whatever animal used to live in this part of the zoo. It was more than likely that the animal escaped back when the zoo was first abandoned and the acid wore away the bars of the enclosure. Not that freedom would have prolonged the poor creature's life. Still, it didn't hurt to check.

It hadn't come across another living being in so long that Me was willing to explore any decrepit ruins for the chance of finding a mere suggestion of life. Half-eaten food, trash, the bones from discarded limbs. The pain of loneliness overshowed the constant physical pain that punctuated daily life.

Me rocked up onto its hands and knees and crawled a few feet further into the enclosure. Bits of flesh from its blistered bare skin stuck to the muddy earth and left a trail of gore leading back to the dominoes. One useless stump of a leg wagged behind as it crawled.

The foot was long gone, lost in the remains of a crumbling shopping mall. Searching for other survivors in the early years, Me spent a lot of time in malls. They were places to find food, clothing, and suggestions of humanity, even though it was all acid-eaten. Back then, Me was bolder in its searches and still held on to hope. Hope it wasn't alone. Hope a solution to the harsh environmental changes might yet exist.

Then its foot got caught in an unmoving escalator. Acid worn stairs that were once mechanized. The corrosive damage to its own body meant Me's foot snapped off cleanly. Pain was still a new enough experience then to cause Me to cry out. Its voice echoed through the remains of the mall as if to emphasize the bleak emptiness. Me bit their tongue till it bled and choked down its cries when it forced the fresh stump out into the rain to cauterize the wound.

"No pain, no gain. Except in the rain."

Throughout the trek across the enclosure, Me stopped only once to cough up blood. Its vision was hazy, but Me thought it spotted a pile of bones hidden beneath what once could have been a sizeable chunk of granite. The top of the stone was still liquid and bubbling from the last downpour of acid rain. With a grunt that sounded more like a barking cough Me dragged itself closer.

It saw the enemy.

"Bad!" It hissed.

Digging its cracked nails deep into the ground, burning off more flesh from its fingers, Me grabbed a clump of mud and flung it at the unassuming purple flower. It missed, and the flower swayed in the breeze, unbothered.

"No! Bad flower!"

As if triggered by the noise, the flower opened up towards the sky and released a plume of pollen. Dusty and grey, the breeze carried it up and away where it would be absorbed by the looming clouds.

"Bad!"

Screaming, crying, with bitter mucus dribbling into its open mouth, Me shuffled back the way it came. No bone was worth that much trouble. Another rumble of thunder sounded in the distance.

"Bad, bad..." Me whimpered. It picked up the pace, crawling as fast as its worn-out body would allow.

Thunder roared overhead with the promise of an imminent downpour. Me crawled faster.

With a dull snap, its wrist gave out and Me tumbled face first into the ground. The acid-soaked mud burned its eye and lips, but it was the pain in its wrist that made Me see stars. Hanging on by a loose thread of tendon was a now useless hand. Me tried to wiggle its fingers to no avail.

Whimpering like a caged animal, it sat up in the mud and took hold of the hand. Me was not strong, not anymore, but there was not much force required to wrench the dangling appendage from the now throbbing arm. Me only needed one hand to play dominoes anyway. It tossed the thing away, forgetting about the need for a piece of bone.

Me sulked back to the game, unaware of the brownish blood dripping from its fresh stump, and took a seat beside the dominoes. With fingers raised, it went to make the next move but stopped.

"Lost?"

Me examined the pieces carefully, lowering its face to the ground as if to kiss it.

"Lost..." it said in awe.

After so many games to determine its fate, so many weeks spent crawling from abandoned place to abandoned place, so many days in search of other living beings, Me lost the game. It shivered out of both fear and relief.

Cackling and crying, Me flung itself down on top of the dominoes. Some clung to its soggy skin as it hobbled back up onto its aching knees and dragged itself out into the open. Face wet with salty tears that stung its raw and skinless face, Me rolled onto its back and exposed its breast to the sky. Thunder ricocheted off the battered walls of the enclosure in response.

There were already patches of skin missing on its chest, exposing acid-stained muscle and bone. Me dug its fingers into the holes and started tearing. Slow work with only one hand. But the rain was coming and would help speed up the process. Death would be slow and agonizing, but at least it would offer that sweet, long-awaited release.

Sizzling filled the air as the first few drops of rain scorched everything within reach. Bubbles formed on every surface. The howling began.

Clog

"**J**esus *Christ!*"

No one else heard the subsequent blasphemies Ned spat into the cabinet encasing his head. The tenants weren't home. That was part of the problem.

"A clog? Sure, no problem. I'll be right over. What part of the house?"

"No idea," said the landlord over the phone.

"What do you mean? Your tenants didn't tell you which drain? Is it in a sink?" Ned prayed it was a sink.

"I don't know. They sent me an email informing me of a clog, and I called you right away. What does it matter?"

Ned sighed, massaging his temples with one hand while holding the phone in the other.

"I guess it don't. I'll be right over."

And now, in this empty row house, he was crawling under cabinets and around toilets, peeking his head into drains and bowls, trying to locate the mystery blockage. In each room he visited, the pipes groaned through the walls, accompanying Ned's grumbling.

"Where in the hell is the sonofabitch?"

Still rubbing his head, Ned surveyed the kitchen and spotted the door.

"Ah, the basement! Gotta be the washer or utility sink. Why didn't they Goddamned say so?"

He pulled at the door, and it lurched out at him as it became unstuck from the frame. The dampness in the air hit him, along with a dank, mildewy odour.

"Clog my ass. More like a flood."

He flicked the switch up and down a few times, but the damp cavern before him remained dark.

"Fan-fuckin-tastic," he said, digging for his flashlight. "Gonna need electrical in here too. These folks sure aren't wasting any time taking care of the place."

As he said it, he turned his attention back to the kitchen, noticing the disarray for the first time. Dirty dishes sat all over the counter, in front of a backsplash painted with the remains of meals from far too long ago.

"Fuckin' animals. No wonder they're having problems."

He trudged down stairs that might as well have been loose planks, keeping his flashlight trained on the concrete below. Ned was acutely aware of the sound of his own breathing.

"Wait a minute," he said, and stopped on the stairs. He held his breath.

The sound of someone breathing filled the darkness.

"Hello? Plumber here. Your landlord sent me about the clog. Anyone down here?"

Nothing answered but the sound of breathing. He shook off a chill.

"Must be the AC," he said to himself.

Thankfully, the utility sink wasn't far from the base of the stairs. Even in the dim light of the flashlight, Ned could pick out the damp spots on the wall behind it. As if anticipating him, the pipes groaned as he stepped closer.

"There you are, you bastard."

Lodged in the drain was a greasy, damp clump of hair that glistened in the light. Holding his flashlight between his teeth,

Ned went right to work. He didn't want to stay in the basement any longer than he needed to.

With a grunt, Ned gave one final pull, and the clump came up in his hands. Something was stuck to the bottom. Still with the flashlight in his mouth, he reached out to touch the mass hanging from the hair but pulled back when he realized it looked a little too much like human flesh.

The pipes groaned again, and Ned jumped. His flashlight hit the wall behind the sink and illuminated the patches of dampness. They were shaped like...faces.

Then one of the damp spots opened its mouth. The others did the same. What had resembled simple water damage in the shadows was now very much alive in the light. Dark, blood-stained teeth dripped with saliva. Thick, grey tongues tasted the air before them. Eyes in rotting sockets followed Ned's every trembling movement.

It wasn't the pipes that were groaning.

Marker

A name is usually the first thing we learn about a person. That's when you meet them, shake their hand, make eye-contact. Within minutes their name has likely vanished from the folds of your brain, and you find yourself having to ask again. That's not what happened when I met Margaret Billings, Artist, 1868 to 1891.

Hers was a name I would never forget.

Despite the age of her grave, her name stood out clearly in the dying light. The stone had not been cleaned or maintained, yet everything was still legible, numbers and letters chiseled to perfection as if she herself supervised the work before her death. Hard to believe an unknown artist who died so young would have such a well-crafted grave marker. Maybe she was one of the lucky ones who snatched up a rich patron or sugar daddy. Or, like me, she had rich family members, and unlike me, they funded her artistic endeavors without question.

Bitch.

I picked her grave because it suited my needs. That she too was an artist was mere coincidence. Years of shifting earth brought about by weather and the passage of time meant her stone marker now tilted back at just the right angle. It made for a perfect backrest as I sat on the soft grass. This part of the cemetery offered the perfect view of the sunset.

"Thanks, Maggie."

Lighting up a cigarette, I began the ritual.

Every time I experienced a depressive episode, which was often, I painted the sunset in cemeteries. The meditative activity brought clarity, and most importantly, money. Goth girls and horror nerds clambered over each other to buy my paintings when I sold them at craft shows.

Before I picked up this unique and financially viable habit, I had brutal artist's block brought on by my unending depression. Months of pain deep in my soul, as I enjoyed melodramatically telling friends over drinks. It earned me laughs and mock sympathy. But a block like that is real. So is the constipation, dizziness, fatigue, tightness in your chest so oppressive you spend each night wondering if you'll die from a heart attack in your sleep. You *are* dying, a little piece at a time.

Then my grandfather died. His death was not caused by creative anxieties. An accountant all his life, he was the furthest thing from creativity, and was not shy about his hatred of me. Although he died five years before, I suspect his soul left his body decades earlier. Greed and spite piloted his withered husk throughout the rest of his obscenely long life.

Standing by his coffin, unmoved, as my mother soaked a box's worth of tissues with her tears, I watched the sunset and inspiration struck. The last, and only, gift my grandfather ever gave me. The pain and blockage went away whenever I thought of him rolling in his grave at the notion of his "useless pansy of a grandchild" earning money doing something he viewed as a waste of time.

"Eat shit," I mumbled as I flicked my brush against the canvas with a flourish. Red acrylic paint splattered the grass like blood.

"Sorry, Maggie," I said without meaning it.

The grave was everything I aimed to avoid. The world never knew the work of Margaret Billings, and it's likely that had nothing to do with her death. Had she achieved artistic greatness, her work would have lived on. Someone other than me would have known her name. Her gravestone would have been surrounded by brightly coloured ribbons and fresh flowers instead of moss and crusty snails. To die unknown meant she only accomplished mediocrity. To call her an artist was an exaggeration.

"Mediocre Maggie," I chuckled.

Once my painting was complete and the cigarette burned down to nothing, I flicked the butt into the grass. The smoke fizzled out but not before leaving a small burned patch around it. That's when I spotted the puddle of orange at my side.

"Ugh, you've got to be kidding me."

Not sure how I managed it, but my only remaining tube of orange paint burst, spilling its guts on the ground. I reached to pick it up to see if there was anything I could salvage. In doing so, the sleeve of my jacket brushed the still damp canvass, smearing my latest creation.

"Are you fucking kidding me!"

With a grunt, I chucked the empty plastic tube across the cemetery. A final splatter of runny paint showered a stone cross engraved with Celtic knots. Somewhere deep in the back of my brain, I heard my grandfather laughing at me. With trembling hands, I cracked the canvas over my knee but succeeded in only breaking the frame. The smeared painting was still whole. The lone eye of the painted sun glared mockingly at me. Failure to destroy my own faulty artwork sent me into a blind rage as I tossed it aside.

"Tut, tut," Grandpa said in my mind. *"Wasting your time as a talentless hack. And the supplies! Waste of money too. Look at*

that mess. You can't even create anything new without mucking it up."

Reaching deep into the warm earth, I pulled up handfuls of grass. The edges of my vision blurred with tears.

"Continue to pursue this nonsense and you will lose everything. Mark my words. This family has no place for frivolity or mediocrity. Stop sulking and get a real job."

I got to my feet without thinking and grabbed my remaining paints. Juggling all the colours, I opened the caps and squeezed.

"So, you want to go insane like that loony who cut off his own ear? Be my guest!"

Colour oozed over my hands, splattering Margaret Billings' tombstone and those of her neighbours in sunset pinks and yellows and purples. All I saw was red. Half-empty tubes lay at my feet like little corpses.

All except one. A tube of golden yellow, held up by a bony hand that squeezed out the last dregs of paint. It oozed down the bones of an arm, shrouded in the tattered remains of what once might have been a sleeve.

Before I could make sense of what was happening, Margaret's head and shoulders were out of the dirt with her hand still held high. After so many years she was little more than bone, but a few stubborn chunks of mouldy flesh still clung to her. Worms wriggled in and out of her sockets, dancing between teeth and ribs. Beetles scuttled across her scalp and through spidery wisps of hair. Eyeless sockets peered at me while I struggled to blink.

When I did, she was further out of the earth. With her hips now free, she used her unencumbered hand to drag herself across the paint-smeared grass as she shook the tube at me with the other.

A growl emanated from deep within her withered larynx, though she said nothing. Not that she needed to.

"S-sorry, M-M-M..."

I stuttered and sputtered like a broken engine. Clenching my fists, I willed myself to call for help, to move, to do anything at all, but I was heavy with...blockage. The weight and pain of my artist's block, now amplified by fear. I would have vomited if I could have forced my mouth open enough.

A scream wrenched out of me when Margaret stood up, trembling on her fleshless legs, and took one step in my direction. With all her remaining strength, she rammed the paint tube into my throat.

The scream in my mouth died before it was fully formed. As I choked on paint and my own blood, the sound was nothing more than a feeble gurgle. A whisper danced into my ear on hot, rancid breath.

"Mediocre?"

You Want One? I'll Give You Five!

There are five reasons nobody goes to the old Cooper place anymore.

• • • •

One: It's not as fun as it used to be.

Neighbourhood kids used to make the long detour on the way home from school to the old house. No one went in. No one would ever dream of going in unless a double-dog-dare was on the table.

Before the accident, if you wanted to improve your skills on the baseball diamond, you went into the Coopers' yard. They always had plenty of stones lying around in the dry grass. And they were always the perfect shape.

One point for hitting the siding. Two points for hitting a window, and a bonus point for breaking it. Just a crack didn't count. The rock had to end up in their living room.

Three points if you hit Mr. or Mrs. Cooper, or one of their ugly kids.

Now, no one dares to throw a stone. Not even if there's a double-dog-dare.

• • • •

Two: It's a safety hazard.

The fire department said they couldn't make it in time. We all saw them watching from the sidewalk that night, but they said it was too late. Better to let it burn for a bit.

Eventually, they doused the whole thing until the charred wood was soggy.

A few kids tried exploring the wreckage, squirming under or jumping over the caution tape. They got in trouble with their parents for doing something so reckless and unsafe.

No one ever got in trouble for starting the fire, though.

• • • •

Three: The smell.

It was worse after the accident. Way worse. The entire town stunk like burning hair for weeks. Now when you walk by, you can catch a faint hint of smoke drifting on the wind. Like the wood is clinging to it and will never let it go.

It's still not as bad as when you stand in the yard or step right up to the house, which you should never do. Then, the house reeks of rotting flesh.

• • • •

Four: The screaming.

You typically hear it in the early evening, right after all the neighbourhood kids should have gotten home from school. But one kid is always missing. One kid never shows up to class the next day. Or the day after.

Our parents try to act like everything's okay, but we know we'll never see those kids again.

There's no more grass surrounding the house. It all burned away, leaving behind soot and ash. The rocks are still all over the yard, but now they're buried under piles of bones. Ribs, and femurs, and child-sized skulls with the meat picked clean.

• • • •

Five: The Coopers didn't die.

Kacie

K acie's locket fell to the floor. Dave checked the box in his arms to make sure he had the right one. Yup, "Dave's Shit" was scrawled angrily across the side. Margo probably hadn't realized that it ended up with his things. He made a mental note to give it to her. That is, if she would let him. Maybe it would be easier to hold onto it.

And yet, he couldn't bring himself to pick it up. There were too many emotions attached to it. Too many memories. But it would be worse to just leave it there. Kacie would be mad if it got scuffed up. Dave forced himself to squat, balancing his "shit" precariously on one arm. Getting back up was harder than he anticipated, however, and he admitted defeat by dropping the box on the floor with a thud. Without staring too long at the necklace and trying to touch it as little as possible, he slipped it into the pocket on his shirt.

That was when the loneliness sank in.

With a sigh, Dave stared at the box at his feet. Trophies of a failed family that had been not-so-lovingly wrapped in newspaper and cardboard. He had no desire to pick it all back up again, so he abandoned it and made his way to the fridge, instead. But it was empty. Of course it was. He stood staring at the blank shelves a moment longer, blinking back tears.

"I'll get groceries tomorrow," he said out loud.

There was no one there to answer him.

After a lonely dinner in a quiet bar, mulling over his regrets and failures, he decided he wasn't ready to go back to the apartment. It wasn't home, and this would be his first time sleeping alone in over twenty years. Reluctantly, he concluded it would be best to take care of the empty fridge first.

Obviously, he bought too much. He was used to shopping for a family of four, and he didn't realize his error until the grocery store was far behind him. When he stared at the now full fridge, he wondered if he would have a chance to eat it all before the mold began to set in. But that was life. Things often had a habit of going bad.

The next day wasn't any easier. With the boxes emptied and stuffed into a corner, and most of his belongings put away, the apartment almost felt like home. But not quite. He missed the ear-splitting noise Ashley made when she played her guitar, the shrill cackles from Kacie as she watched trashy reality TV. Even the barrage of Margo's endless scolding. It was too quiet here.

Insomnia had plagued him on and off the previous night, despite being mentally and physically exhausted from the move. The humming from the fridge was too loud; when it wasn't, his room was too quiet. The bed was cold and empty on one side. He tossed and turned well into the morning. All he wanted to do was leave this lifeless apartment. He wanted to walk right out the door and back into his old life. Another part of him wanted to curl up on the small, second-hand couch in his living room and die. He did neither.

After some time spent staring at the wall, Dave did end up on the couch, where he stared at his phone, instead. He needed to hear their voices. Margo was out of the question. But one of the girls... Kacie. He still had her locket. Quickly, and without thinking, he found her name in his contact list. There was no answer. Of course there wasn't. Dave shook his head and called Ashley, instead. This time, the call connected.

"Hey, Ash. It's Dad." He was surprised she even answered at all. She didn't say anything when she heard his voice. There was only tentative breathing on her end of the line.

"I was unpacking yesterday, and I found Kacie's locket if you-"

There was a brief rustling followed by silence. He didn't blame her for hanging up.

Still on the couch, he obeyed his instinct to curl up. He didn't die like that part of him hoped he would, but he did cry himself to sleep.

The first week at that apartment was only more of the same. Although Dave told himself he had accepted being on his own, he still found it impossible to even lie in the bed by himself. That first night of insomnia was torture compared to the agitated rest he got on the couch. He couldn't handle another restless night. He didn't even want to look at the bedroom anymore and kept the door closed at all times.

The couch was the only way he was guaranteed at least a shred of sleep. It reminded him of taking a power nap before driving one of the girls to soccer or band practice. It made him feel like this quiet, lonely place was only temporary. Until he opened his eyes.

But a week of that feigned normalcy made his back seize during the work day. His neck crackled and crunched whenever he moved his head, and he soon discovered new pain there too. In the middle of the night, after a week of pain and discomfort, he admitted defeat and shuffled his way to the bedroom.

But something wasn't right. There was a shadowy figure on the bed waiting for him. With his heart in his throat, Dave fumbled for the light switch with one hand while rubbing his eyes with the other.

"Who's there? Kacie! How did you get in?"

But when the realization hit, it occurred to him that he didn't actually care how she got in. Only that she was there.

"Kay, you're really here. What *are* you doing here?"

She stared at him with cold, glassy eyes.

"You know why I'm here."

He didn't. He racked his brain, stumbled over syllables, but came up with nothing. It was late, and he was too tired to think. Besides, he knew what Margo was like, especially now. It was likely that Kacie would rather stay with him given the current circumstances.

"I guess I do. Oh, hon, I missed you so much. Why didn't you tell me you were coming?"

Without waiting for an answer, Dave swooped in and wrapped his daughter in a spine crushing hug. He didn't want to let go. Never again. Even though she wasn't hugging him back. But that wasn't important.

"I'm so happy you came to see me. Oh! And I have something for you."

Prying his arms off of Kacie, he reached into the drawer of the bedside table and pulled out the locket.

"I found this with my things." He held it up for her to see.

She didn't even blink.

But Dave didn't let that dampen his excitement. He lifted the locket above Kacie's head and slid the chain down around her neck.

"I'll get that polished for you," he offered. "Professionally. Just for you."

Dave thought back to the day he found it with his things and didn't remember it being in such rough shape then. He was certain the locket caught the light when it fell out of the box on moving day. But, then again, it had been sitting in a drawer since then. And the tarnish was spreading further by the second. Blinking a few times in disbelief, Dave decided it was time for him to go back to sleep and clear his head.

"You just make yourself at home," he said. "The bedroom's yours, if you want it. I'll go back to the couch."

Kacie didn't respond.

She was never this quiet. Something wasn't right. Tentatively, Dave put his hand on her shoulder. She didn't move, and her skin was cold. But she was real, and that was the most important part.

"Do you need any extra blankets? Or I can turn up the heat?"

"I'm fine."

Kacie's eyes narrowed to slits as if she were studying her father, waiting for something. Dave quickly removed his hand from her shoulder.

She probably didn't want to be there, even if he was a better choice than Margo. Not after everything their family had been through. But she was there, and that was all that mattered.

"Sleep if you can, hon. We'll talk in the morning."

But when morning came, Dave convinced himself that it was all a dream. There was no way Kacie was there. It wasn't possible. And yet, he found himself watching for signs of life from the bedroom door as he sat on the couch. He continued to stare at the door from the kitchen as he drank his morning coffee. But he could not open it to check. If he went into the bedroom and she was in there, that was a huge faux pas for any parent of a teenager. And if she wasn't there, and it was just a dream, he was afraid his heart would break. For now, it was easier to leave the door closed as he mulled over the two possible outcomes. Schrödinger's daughter. That one made him laugh. It was the first time he had laughed in months.

The faint squeak of the doorknob put a stop to the laughter as Kacie emerged from the bedroom. Dave was relieved when he realized that he hadn't dreamt the whole thing, but a hint of unease remained in the pit of his stomach when he saw the scowl on Kacie's face. Her eyes were sunken and glassy, but there was a fire burning within them. The tarnish on her locket was much worse in the daylight.

"Sorry, hon. Did I wake you? Did you sleep well?"

The old wooden floor creaked as she walked over to the couch. She never took her eyes off of him.

"I can make more coffee, if you want?" he offered.

"No," she croaked.

Dave put his mug down and made his way into the living room. He stopped a few feet away from the couch. Something about the way her jaw clenched and her eyes narrowed told him to keep his distance.

"Listen, I know things haven't been easy, particularly between me and your mother, but we'll get through this. I promise. It's just... a bump in the road. We can get through this. You and me. So, if you want to talk about anything, I'm here."

Dave clenched and unclenched his hands while he waited for Kacie to respond.

"But if you just need your space, I won't bother you. Okay?"

The rest of her body remained rigid as her neck hinged to allow a slight nod. Dave's hands relaxed, although the rest of his body didn't.

God, she looked awful. Had she slept at all? He almost clenched his hands again when he thought about all she had been through. But he pushed those thoughts away. He didn't want to think about the past anymore. He wasn't ready to face it. And he was happy to see Kacie, no matter how uncomfortable he felt right now.

"I'm glad you're here, hon. I really am." He couldn't be sure if he was telling her or himself. Her response settled the debate.

"Does it make you feel less guilty?"

"Kay, your mother and I tried to..." He choked back the lump in his throat and took a deep breath. "Yes. I guess it does make me feel less guilty."

"You don't deserve that peace of mind."

"Why would you say that?"

The sneer on her lips was answer enough, and Dave's skin crawled. He needed to get away from her. Most importantly, he wanted to be free from the guilt.

"I have to go to work."

He was ready for work and out the door before Kacie even had a chance to get up from the couch. But when he came home at the end of the day, she was still sitting there, and the guilt was still with him, deep in the pit of his stomach.

Slowly, and without moving the rest of her body, Kacie pulled her head away from the window and fixed her gaze on her father when he came through the door. Without reacting, she watched him hold up the take-out bag from her favourite burger place. Dave was beaming, or at least faking it, but all she did was glare at him.

So much for being a good father, he thought. He wondered why he even bothered. But he was happy to have her there all the same and hoped her mood would improve once she started eating. At least, that's what he kept telling himself.

As Dave unpacked the food onto the kitchen counter, he became aware of an unusual smell. It was something rotten. Or worse. He sniffed the take-out bag, but all he smelled was burger grease. Next, he checked the garbage bin under the sink, but even when he stuck his head in, he couldn't pinpoint the scent. Then the fridge, convinced that the large grocery haul had finally gone bad. That wasn't it either. He thought to ask Kacie about it but decided that was not the best place to start the conversation. The smell was a problem for later.

"You hungry? I got your favourite."

If she even bothered to answer, he didn't hear her. But he hadn't expected a response, anyway. He brought the food over to the couch and squeezed in beside her. Despite the awkwardness and Kacie's bad mood, Dave had actually missed her. He found himself glancing at his watch far too often throughout the workday.

After placing the foil wrapped burger in Kacie's lap, Dave tore into his meal without a second to waste. He could taste the nostalgia and instantly felt better. There was an ember of hope in Dave's heart now that he was leaving that lonesome week behind.

That hope sank into the pit of his stomach, upsetting the burger digesting there, when he glanced at Kacie and saw that she wasn't enjoying this moment as much as he was. Not only was she not eating, but she was glaring at him, wide-eyed, nostrils flared. Dave had never seen her that angry before, not even when Ashley had spilled soda on her laptop. He didn't want to admit it, but he was afraid of her.

"Kay? Everything alright? Are you not hungry?"

"No. Not hungry," she said through clenched teeth.

He wanted to get away from her again. Every muscle in his body was tense, screaming at him to run.

"I'll put yours in the fridge for later."

Dave shot his hand into her lap, grabbing the burger quickly and trying not to touch her. Once he was off the couch, he charged into the kitchen. His heart was pounding, and a knot in his gut told him that he would not be finishing the rest of his burger any time soon. He tossed both burgers back into their bag and shoved them into the fridge.

This was crazy. He was afraid of his own daughter. Dave knew to give teenagers a wide berth when they were in a mood, but this was more than just a mood. But, he tried to reason with himself as he washed his hands and face in the kitchen sink, she had been through hell. The whole family had. Now was not the time for him to be distancing himself from her. But when he lifted his head and caught her glaring at him again, his courage and fatherly love went down the drain.

"I was thinking of going out for a walk since it's so nice out. Care to join me?" He hoped she didn't hear the tremble in his voice. More importantly, he hoped she would say no.

"You go," she croaked. "I'll stay here."

Dave thought he caught the ghost of a smile on her lips, and it brought shivers down his spine. But he was relieved.

"Alright, hon. See you in a bit."

In his eagerness to get out of the cramped apartment, the door slammed behind him too loudly. His first thought was that he had disturbed the neighbours. He didn't take Kacie into consideration until he was out of the building. Even though it probably made him a bad father, he didn't care at all if she took offence. She was the reason he needed to get out in the first place.

But the farther he got away from his apartment, the more he told himself that he wasn't just a bad father, he was a horrible one. Dave argued with himself, repeating over and over in his mind that he shouldn't be running from her. He shouldn't be afraid of her. Kacie was clearly still struggling, after all this time. So was he. And they were doing it alone. That was only making the problem worse. After the incident, all four members of their little family had shut down and sequestered themselves from one another. How could any of them expect to heal?

Dave barely reached the nearby park when he decided he needed to do better. The roller coaster of emotions he'd been experiencing since Kacie's unexpected reappearance in his life was no excuse, and separating himself from her wouldn't solve anything. It hadn't worked with Margo and Ashley. He and Kacie wouldn't be able to heal properly if they didn't work together.

He marched back to the apartment with a newfound determination to start behaving like a better father. He was going to be there for his daughter when she needed him. Whether he liked it or not.

That determination vanished the moment he got back.

The rotting stench was far more potent than it had been when he left, and his gag reflex jumped into action. The bedroom, bathroom, and closet doors were all wide open, and so were all the kitchen cabinets and cupboards. Dave hadn't taken much with him when Margo asked him to leave, but each and every one of his few belongings was strewn about the floor of the living room. He blinked a few times, unsure whether this was real or not. How could such a big mess be made in such a short amount of time?

Kacie was sitting in the middle of the destruction, legs splayed out like a broken ragdoll. Her head was tilted at an uncomfortable angle as she flipped through the fifteen-month planner that Dave used for work. When she made eye contact with him, she bared her teeth in a grin and flopped back onto the floor. Her head landed with a thud, but the deranged smile remained.

"What the hell, Kacie! What is this? How did you...? Why? I just came back to... I'm going out again, and this mess better be cleaned up by the time I'm back!"

This time, he slammed the door intentionally. As he clenched his trembling hands into fists, he told himself that he was furious with her. But deep down, he knew he was actually afraid.

Dave let his legs carry him all the way to the park. They were shaking so much he was surprised they even supported his body at all. Each time he wiped the clammy sweat from his brow, it reappeared.

It was too much. Kacie sprawled out on the floor like that, just like the night all of this started. He tried to shake away the mental image. Did she make that mess to punish him? To hurt him? To feed his guilt? He should be happy that one of his daughters chose be around him right now. Grateful, even. But

Kacie hadn't even been with him twenty-four hours and was making him miserable. Fatherhood was supposed to be hard, but not like this.

Ignorant of how crazed he appeared to onlookers, Dave paced around the park, mumbling to himself, trying to rationalize her recent behaviour. She was not herself. And maybe she never would be again. What had happened to Kacie was... Well, it was so awful that he still refused to think about it. He still would not allow himself to dwell on that night. It was horrible. It was downright traumatic.

He stopped, and all of his muscles released their tension. Yes, it was traumatic. No family should have to go through that. No parent should have to bury their child.

The memories came rushing in. A year's worth of pain came crashing down on his shoulders. His skin prickled with the wave of realization, and he let his feet carry him to the nearest trashcan. As his stomach heaved, he decided that he would throw out the half-eaten burger in the fridge at home.

He wanted so desperately for everything to be as it once was that he was ignoring what was going on in front of him. No good would come from his continued suppression of the events of the past year. And it wasn't doing him or Kacie any good, either.

Collapsing onto the adjacent park bench, Dave placed his head in his hands and let the sobs come. He hated himself for his part in all of this. Margo convinced him that what happened to their family was entirely his fault, and he allowed himself to agree with her. He had taken on a family's worth of guilt and sadness and let it fester until Margo and Ashley had no choice but to get rid of him. But now there was a chance to make things right, and he was failing. Maybe there had never been any hope of succeeding in the first place.

Kacie was not okay, she might never be, and Dave didn't know how to help her. He wanted her back in his life – he wanted Margo and Ashley back too – but he didn't know if it was possible anymore. Dave didn't know if he would ever be a good father again, or if he had even been a good father to begin with. His ex-wife would attest that he certainly hadn't been a good husband. Even though he thought he tried his best, everything had still turned to shit. His eldest daughter hated him, his wife wanted a divorce, and his youngest was... She needed help. *He* needed help. But who could he turn to? Who could possibly help right now?

When the tears stopped and the lamps in the park flickered to life, he decided that he didn't need to have all the answers right away. The first step was simply to be a good father and talk to Kacie. They could work things out from there and figure it out together. Surely, there must be someone out there who knew how to help their family heal and move past this. Someone who knew how to help Kacie.

Whether he wanted to or not, Dave needed to go back to her. He had to make things right somehow. He had to try.

When he got home, Dave didn't want to open the door. He contemplated clamping his eyes shut as he entered. But there was no need. The apartment was as empty as he was used to seeing it. The mess was mostly gone, save for the usual pile of boxes in the corner that were now covered in mold. One lone item laying in the middle of the living room, and it stank of mildew. It was his work planner, and it was open to the date from exactly one year ago. Of course it was.

There was no sign of his daughter, but Dave knew she was there. As he approached the bedroom door, the ever-increasing stench of rot assaulted his nostrils once more.

"Kacie?"

While waiting for an answer he tried his best not to vomit again. But she never spoke. The only sound was a peculiar shuffling from the other side of the door, like she was at least willing to come close enough to listen. Or like a pacing animal, sizing up its prey.

"Thank you for tidying up. And I'm sorry for yelling. I'm here if you need to talk. I want to help you."

There was no answer, but he knew she was in there all the same. For now, he was content to leave her alone. He wanted to be there for her if she needed him, but he didn't want to see her emerge from the bedroom. If he could barricade the door and trap her in there forever, that would suit him just fine. All he wanted was to keep her close, but from a distance. Despite his revelation in the park, he didn't have the courage to face his daughter just yet. He busied himself around the apartment instead.

With trembling hands, Dave reached into the fridge and pulled out the leftover burgers. The bag was unusually heavy. He dropped it immediately after peeking inside. Hardly any food remained. Handfuls of maggots had taken their place. Trying his best not to look at their fat, greasy bodies, he plucked the bag off the floor with his fingertips and tossed it in the garbage bin. As the bag landed at the bottom, a swarm of flies rose up into Dave's face. He leaned over the sink to vomit again, but only brought up bile. It was only when he finished gagging that he saw the rust on the faucet and the mold peeking up from the grout between the tiled counter.

"Kacie," he said with his face still in the sink. His own trembling voice echoed in his ears. "Hon. We need to talk. Can you come out here, please?"

The buzzing of the flies was all he heard while he listened for an answer that never came.

"I can wait. I've got all night."

With a sigh, Dave shuffled over to the couch and sat down, keeping the bedroom door in his line of sight. He thought his nerves alone would keep him from sleeping for the foreseeable future, but he surprised himself when he jerked awake from an uncomfortable position.

It was dark outside, and the only light in the apartment came from the streetlamp beside the window. The mold spread from the boxes in the corner and grew up the wall, eating away at the old wallpaper. His ceiling was damp and dripping, and the flies multiplied until they drowned out the sounds of passing cars. Maggots flailed over one another on the window ledge. The ones that tumbled to the floor burrowed under the now-loose and mildewed floorboards. The stench of decayed flesh was nauseating.

But the state of his apartment was the least of his worries. Dave's heart leapt into his throat when he noticed Kacie standing over the couch. Her locket was tarnished beyond recognition, and she was holding a large, rusty knife.

Now that Dave had experienced his moment of mental clarity in the park, and the joy of having his daughter back in his life had worn off, he saw her as she was. She was nothing like the daughter he remembered.

Her body zigzagged where her shattered hip and legs prevented her from standing completely straight, and her head tilted off to one side where her neck was broken. The side of her head that hit the pavement a year ago was still slick with blood that glistened in the light of the streetlamp, and the skull beneath it was caved in. Any scratches and bruises that had once been present were now overshadowed by patches of rot. And where it was most aggressive, the skin was peeling, exposing bone and equally rotten muscle underneath. The only part of her that had any life at all were her eyes, and they burned with ferocity, glowing orange in the lamp light.

Dave clenched his hands. He knew what to do.

"Do you want to talk about that night?"

"What were you doing out that was so important?" Her voice was like a death rattle.

"I was coming home from work late. My car broke down."

"You think I believe that?"

The knife flashed in the dark as it picked up the light from the street lamp.

"Kacie, why were you out in the middle of the road?"

"Don't try to place the blame on me! You did this."

"But I didn't," said Dave, admitting it more to himself than her.

"You did!"

The knife was closer now, hovering above his head.

"No. I wasn't driving the car."

Kacie faltered only briefly, but her eyes narrowed and she gripped the knife tightly.

"Liar! You were *there*. I *saw* you."

"I was there, yes. But your mother was behind the wheel, not me."

"No."

Again, the knife flashed, but it trembled in Kacie's bony fingers.

"Yes. I know this hurts to hear, but your mother and I were having problems long before that night. We love each other, we do, but we've never been good for one another."

"Stop trying to distract me!"

"Kacie, you need to listen," he said with surprising firmness. "I was working late that night, and my car wouldn't start. After the tow truck brought me to the repair shop, I called your mother to explain the situation and to tell her that I would be home even later. She was furious. I thought she was going to..."

He glanced nervously at the knife.

"I thought she was going to kill me. She was mad at me for not taking better care of the car, for not keeping on top of any problems, for wasting time. Whatever excuses she came up with to yell at me. You know she never needs a reason."

"But she would never."

The knife lowered by a fraction.

"She didn't want me spending the extra money on a cab home, so she told me she'd come and get me. I honestly think she wanted a chance to do her worst without you and your sister around. But that's what did it. She turned to look at me, to yell at me, and took her eyes off the road. And it was dark. And she... We didn't see you. Not until it was too late."

The knife was almost at Kacie's side, but Dave kept his eye on it in case it decided to spring back up.

"I didn't see her," said Kacie.

"No. She was in shock. She got out of the car but froze the moment she saw you. I was the one who sprang into action because... Well, I don't know. I don't even remember getting out of the car."

Dave shifted his gaze from the knife to his daughter's eyes.

"You were gone before I even got the 911 operator on the phone."

The knife was still firmly within Kacie's grasp, but it had dropped all the way to her crooked side.

As his fists unclenched, Dave let out a louder sigh than he anticipated.

"Kacie, I'm so sorry. You're right, I do feel guilty about what happened. And even though I wasn't the one driving the car, I'm not entirely innocent either. I've experienced a lot of hatred towards your mother this past year – and God knows we made things worse for Ashley – but I've forgiven Margo. And I've forgiven myself, even if no one else has. All three of you are the most important people in the world to me, and I just want a chance to be a family again. Kacie, whatever you need to do to find peace, I'll help you. Whatever it takes, I will be there for you. And you can stay with me as long as you need to. I just want you to be happy."

"No," croaked Kacie.

"No?"

She limped towards the front door and tightened her grip on the knife.

"Kay, what are you doing?"

He heard only one broken foot dragging across the floor.

"Where are you going, hon? Can't you stay? Kacie?"

The sound of shuffling stopped and the door clicked open before the light from the hallway entered the dark apartment, illuminating the places where mold and maggots should have been. Kacie's head turned and lolled over her shoulder, hanging sideways. Her face was obscured in shadow, but her eyes still shone brightly, like those of a cat.

"Where are you going?" Dave insisted "You can't leave now."

She stared at him in the dark.

"I'm going to visit Mother."

The door slammed behind her and the apartment was plunged into darkness once more.

Dave wanted to call out to her not to leave him again, but there was no point. She was already gone.

Cold Cuts & Cigarettes

B ob's funeral is a disaster before it's even begun. Dad is
sitting in a corner, staring at his beer, fighting back
emotions he pretends he doesn't have. Dad's new fling, an
out-of-towner named Trish, is running around, fussing over
every little detail. I drift from room to room, trying to stay out
of everyone's way and trying harder to remain unseen.

Trish still doesn't understand how things are done around
here, but she's trying, and she's making a mess of everything.
She wants to prove she can fit in, although I can't imagine why.
Maybe she sought this place out because she too is dying a
slow and meaningless death. Maybe she didn't know any better
and thought this was a quaint place to retire. I don't like her.
I haven't liked any of the girlfriends that have come and gone
since Mom's funeral, mostly because they were all women from
town. Women who used to be Mom's friends. At least I don't
have that kind of history with Trish. At least Dad married this
one.

Neighbours are trickling in, filling the place with a hum of
murmurs and condolences. Some have brought their children
along, teenagers who still look far too young. This will be their
first. First funeral, and first time seeing our town for what it
really is.

Mom's was my first. I wish it had been a stranger like it
will be for these kids. Bob was the kind of small-town fixture
that everyone knew by sight, but who no one really *knew*. This
new batch of first timers might have nightmares for the first
few weeks afterwards, but they won't carry around the same

kind of trauma that I do. They'll be numb to it all by the time they attend their third funeral. By their fifth, these kinds of community gatherings will be an accepted way of life. Somewhere around the eighth is usually when the existential crisis kicks in.

I left town after my twelfth.

Things are oddly calm in the now cramped house, but Trish's constant worrying is adding an undercurrent of pandemonium that everyone is only peripherally aware of. Things on her list aren't going according to plan. Dani is nowhere in sight, and a platter of cold cuts is missing. Not that anyone other than Trish noticed either of these things. I wonder how long she'll stick with Dad after this funeral is over.

Bob would have hated being here. All the noise, all the people, all the chaos. Good thing he's dead, I guess.

I suppose I should call him Uncle Bob, but we were never that close. We could have been, but no one in my family ever learned how to cope with their feelings. He wanted to keep to himself in the confines of his living room, and I wanted to get the hell out of town. Same thing. But when I moved back home at the start of the new year, neither one of us made any effort to have a relationship. I can't remember the last time I saw him in person. It's no one's fault. That's just how it is sometimes.

"Is Dani on her way?" asks Trish. Her voice is quiet, but the nervous tremor is audible over the din.

God I want a cigarette. It's too hot in here with all the bodies crammed into such a small space. My skin is burning and I can't stop thinking about how much I want to smoke. But it's a city habit I'm trying to break. That only makes the need worse.

I only started smoking out of boredom. And loneliness, and uncertainty, and fear. But it never dulled my emotions the way I hoped it would and, a coward in all aspects of life, I couldn't bring myself to try something stronger. Besides, this town has enough stigma surrounding carcinogens to begin with, and I can't give the neighbours another reason to gossip about me right now.

"I'm going to step outside," I say without answering her.

She's too busy, too flustered, to mind. She moves on to the next poor soul, asking about Dani like that's the only thing on her frazzled mind.

Things aren't any better outdoors. It's that rancid part of spring where the snow is all gone but the air is still a touch too cold and the stench of rot still lingers from the thaw. Oh well, as long as the ground's not still frozen.

"Hey, loser," a voice croaks from the driveway.

It's Dani. Finally.

As she makes her way towards me, all I'm aware of are thick, round, black sunglasses that cover her eyes completely. I doubt that anyone will see a suggestion of her eyes today. The glasses hide the signs of heavy drinking, or maybe a late-night working. Or perhaps one of her on-again-off-again partners hit her. Again. However, no one else at the funeral is sporting a black eye, so it can't be that. Dani has never been one to back down from a fight. Win or lose, she goes down swinging.

And then I realize there might be another explanation. I'm embarrassed it didn't occur to me first. Maybe, just maybe, she has been crying about the death of our uncle and the glasses are hiding how puffy and swollen her eyes are. But I'll never ask her if it's true. Like my dad and his brother, Dani and I are close only at a distance.

"How is he?" she asks once she's near enough to touch.

"Ask him yourself," I say, and my hands end up in my pockets.

"And Trish?" This time, there's less concern in her voice.

"Confused," I say. "Stressed. She still doesn't understand why we do the wake first and the burial second. And apparently a platter of cold cuts is missing. As if there isn't enough food here."

Dani shrugs. "Well, the McMillans are coming. Hell, they might be the ones behind the missing food."

That gets a smile out of me. Dani only half smiles before adjusting her dress and stepping past me.

"Did Dad buy the good pickles? The kind Grandad liked?"

"Trish did the shopping. You'll have to ask her."

"Shit. She probably got something gross like bread-and-butter instead of gherkins."

With a sigh (and possibly her trademark eyeroll, although I can't tell behind the sunglasses), Dani steps into the house and is immediately absorbed by the other mourners. Her voice changes, and the tone that carries through the house and outside is that of a grieving relative. What an actress. She would have been better suited to the city than me. She's resilient and can fit in with any crowd. Her coping strategies are more self-destructive than mine, but she survives it all better than I ever could. If there's any fear in her, she never shows it. But unlike me, she won't dare leave town. She's loyal. And she's not afraid of death.

Hands still in my pockets, I clench the carton there. It's empty, save for a single cigarette that's mangled now that it's been bounced around from pocket to pocket and squeezed for comfort. But I don't dare check. If I see it, no matter what state it's in, I'll smoke it. I can't do that. Not now. If I do, then I'll be forced to buy another pack. And then I'll never be able to bring myself to quit. I'm saving this last one. I don't know what for, though. Maybe Dad's funeral? But that could be a long way off. Or not. You never know. Especially around here.

I wonder how Trish will cope with that one. She won't. It'll be up to me to take charge. The eldest child. The only boy. But I was a city boy. For a while at least. Dani stayed. She's the one the community will trust to make sure everything goes as planned. She's been to more funerals than I have. She's never faltered.

There's a clang at the end of the lane, and I lock eyes with an embarrassed looking teenager. The undertaker steps out from behind one of the houses, his apron covered in blood and something greenish-brown. He glares at the kid, and opens his mouth to yell, but he spots me out of the corner of his eye and stops. With only a slight nod, he acknowledges me, wordlessly offering his condolences for my loss, and scoops up a heap of dropped tools before disappearing.

They're preparing my uncle.

My stomach churns when Trish's voice echoes out that she found the missing platter of cold cuts. It was in the kitchen with the other back-up trays. Of course. I've never seen her this flustered before, but a funeral around here is a lot to deal with. Too much, in fact.

I understand why we need to eat before the funeral, but I don't know how anyone can. Bob must be split open right now, dripping into metal buckets, looking like a tray of cold cuts himself. They're pulling out his organs and cataloguing them. Maybe the teenager, clearly an apprentice, slips and drops my uncle's greasy liver on the floor. Does it bounce? Or does it fall with a splat, losing its shape and becoming a puddle?

My gut heaves and I clutch the cigarette carton once more. I taste bile at the back of my tongue.

Something brushes against my leg and I jump, heart in my throat, stars in my eyes. An image of Uncle Bob's hand wrapping around my ankle flashes through my mind.

It's just a cat. Minnie, the neighbourhood stray. Everyone feeds her, but no one owns her. With her snaggle toothed smile, she's friendlier than she looks.

"Hey, Miss." I reach down and pet her, and she raises her head to meet my palm. She's softer than she has any right to be, but she's not much to look at. Jagged teeth peek out from between her lips, and her bright eyes are obscured behind a fan of gnarled whiskers. Tumours cluster on her back, creating bulges in her mottled fur.

"Keeping tabs on everyone?"

She chirrups in response. What I really want to ask is how is she still alive after all she's been through? How can she survive here when the people can't? Her purring slows my heartrate but doesn't calm my nerves. I might need a couple of beers for that. Maybe more.

"You're lucky you don't have to go through this," I say to her.

With a flick of her tail, she chirrups again and I understand the real reason she's shown up.

"Alright, alright. Give me a minute."

I peek through the door like I don't want to be seen, then slip inside after confirming that all eyes are on Dad in his corner. Head down, slinking in between black clad bodies, I make my way to the food table.

"It's so good he's back," I hear someone say in a soft voice across the room. "He's been gone too long."

They're talking about me. All day, people have treated me like I've only returned for the funeral, when in reality I've been home for months. But if Minnie didn't get the memo, then perhaps I hid myself away a little too well. Just like Uncle Bob.

I load the plate with meats and cheeses, reminiscing on the soul-crushing shame that accompanied my return into town. I couldn't survive on my own in the city. It was all too much. Too loud. Too many people. And then there were the what ifs. What if I died the same way that Mom and Uncle Bob did? The same way that everyone in this town died. Would anyone even bury me the right way?

The loneliness got me in the end. No one understood my relationship with death. And they could never understand my fears. As I moved from place to place, trying to fit in, trying to find peace, the only constant was my smoking addiction. I couldn't take it anymore. After years of trying, I slunk back home with my tail between my legs and hid myself away in the darkest corners of Dad's house.

But I can't survive here either. I'm nothing like Minnie. She's resilient, and ancient. And loved. The neighbours won't care for me the way they care for her. Not unless I can purge the image of a city boy from their minds. I abandoned them for a place that doesn't understand our way of life and death. And they don't care that I left the city for that very reason. They don't care that I regret my decision. I should never have left in the first place.

This plate of food should be for me, for the guests. We need our energy. But Minnie is a guest too, I suppose. Everyone is on a first name basis with her, and like us she visits every funeral. She knows the town and its secrets better than the oldest council members. She sees everything as she slinks between the streets on her daily wanderings. Besides, I don't have the stomach for food right now, and there's no sense letting this all go to waste.

I slip back out the way I came and Minnie is waiting for me by the door. Her paws stay planted outside the threshold. She's not the kind of cat to shy away from treats or attention, but she respects boundaries. Minnie doesn't go into places that don't belong to her. With one exception. She will only enter a home when she smells imminent death. You can tell that the tumours have reached their final, lethal stage when Minnie shows up in your house. If relatives are nearby in another room, she might let out a meow to alert them. They'll only have about an hour or so to pass the body off to the undertaker before the corpse starts to become dangerous.

Unlike me, Minnie is a good neighbour. She's always looking out for us. They say she was in Bob's kitchen when he died, curled up on his lap. He would have died alone if it weren't for her.

"As promised."

She's polite enough to wait until the paper plate touches the porch before she lowers her head and eats like she hasn't already been given a dozen snacks since morning. Minnie slurps at the pâté and my stomach churns as I think of Uncle Bob again. She glances up at me as if to confirm that she doesn't have to share, and I push the plate a little closer to her.

I take the cigarette carton out of my pocket and open it. The cigarette inside is mangled, as expected, but still useable. I don't have a lighter in my pockets, but Trish must keep a box of matches somewhere.

"How do you do it, Min? Huh? How can you stand it here?"

She snaps at a piece of cheese without looking at me, although her ears twitch in my direction. I stroke her back again and the purring resumes.

"I don't even know why I came back. It was all just... I was scared in the city but... but I'm scared here too. I don't..." I chuckle. "I guess I'm not cut out to live anywhere. You need to share some tips with me, Min."

We sit together while the sounds of the wake drone on behind us. Hushed voices all telling the same lies about how much Bob will be missed. How important he was to the community. They all seem to forget he was a shut-in who rarely left the house. He only went out for beer and funerals.

When the paper plate is empty, licked clean and only a little soggy in a handful of places, Minnie nudges my arm with her head before taking her leave. She doesn't look back. I suppose, according to local superstition, that's a good thing. If Minnie looks back at you, she's likely to see the Grim Reaper looming over your shoulder.

"Your date over?" asks Dani.

I turn quickly, but I'm not entirely surprised to find her standing in the doorway.

"I guess it is. How are you surviving?"

She shrugs.

"And Trish?"

"Nervous. She doesn't get it. Keeps asking me why we can't get it over with. She won't dare ask anyone else, though."

I stare at the cigarette carton in my hands.

"Need me to talk to her?"

"No."

"Sure?"

"You missed the last three funerals," she says. I have a hard time reading her face under those glasses.

"So? I've been to all the others since I turned 18."

"But you missed three."

I scoff. "They weren't even relatives."

"No, they were your neighbours. Annie Grace Jones, Maureen Beech, and Old Man Hiebert. You knew them. All of them. They would have done anything for you, but you couldn't be there for them."

I flounder. "What's the big deal? It's only three!"

Her jaw clenches.

"Come on. You're acting like I'm as bad as Trish."

"You're sitting out here alone while everyone is inside grieving together."

"I wasn't alone," I say, my voice just above a whisper. My eyes search for Minnie, but she's gone.

"You've changed."

"No, I haven't."

"Trish may not understand why we do this, but at least she participates."

"For fuck's sake."

"*You left!*"

"But I came back."

Dani takes a deep breath. "But you still left."

"Well, I'm here now."

"Are you?"

She disappears into the house before I can come up with an answer. Against my better judgement, I slip the carton back in my pocket and follow her.

The black mass that fills the house is overwhelming. It's worse this time now that I don't have a clear mission. And I swear there are more people than before. I only half recognize the faces in front of me. But they all know exactly who I am, and the coldness in their eyes tells me they feel the same way about my departure as Dani.

I decide making my way back to the food table is the safest option, although I don't have the stomach for it. Everything laid out in the meticulously planned spread makes me think of my uncle. I think back to the undertaker and his inexperienced assistant. What are they doing to Bob right at this moment?

My head fills with the sound of cracking ribs and I envision the undertaker, elbow deep in Bob's chest, as he roots around for a shrunken and rotted heart. Pickled onions in jars line stainless steel shelves, looking like olives. Slices of the bladder are laid out on a tray with bits of intestines on the side like peperoni. A pâté of liver is smeared across the glass plate of a microscope. In the end, we're all just a platter of cold cuts for the undertaker.

Bile rises in my throat once more and I put back the paper plate.

"I need a drink," I mutter only to myself, and pat the cigarette carton in my pocket for good measure.

Dad has migrated to the kitchen now, and it feels out of place to see him out of his corner and on his feet. But this is where the beer is kept, and he would never ask someone to grab him a fresh drink when he has two legs that work perfectly fine. I squeeze him on the shoulder and he nods without looking at me. In his peripheral, I could be anyone. He's got so much on his mind he's probably forgotten he has children. At least with the way Trish hovers around him, it's likely he hasn't forgotten about his wife. Or maybe she's just another face to him right now.

"Hang in there, Dad," I say awkwardly as I pass by. He sips his beer.

I grab my own beer and bring the bottle to my lips before the cap hits the counter.

"Take it easy, sport," says someone who could be Mr. Allen from down the street. Between the beer and, well, everything, all the faces have started to blur together. Or maybe I've been away too long and no one is familiar to me anymore.

"You don't want to be falling over tonight," the potential Mr. Allen continues. "I've seen more than a few take a tumble into an open grave, and it's never pretty. But then again, you're too young to remember the last double funeral."

He laughs like that's some kind of joke. I grimace and bring the bottle to my lips again, drinking down the nausea.

Once he leaves the kitchen, his own beer nestled in his fist, I feel a hand on my arm and a small voice in my ear.

"Does it help?" asks Trish. Her voice is trembling, and the good (albeit high-strung) hostess façade is no longer apparent.

I lock eyes with her, thinking back to the time we buried Alice Schaffer. It was... messy. Without a word, I hand her a bottle.

She offers a weak smile as thanks. "I'll make sure I don't... I won't fall into the grave," she promises.

Then she's gone. And it's just me and Dad in the kitchen. The wake continues on without us as we drink our beer in silence. The hum of voices through the closed door is like the static on Grandad's old TV set. I almost reach for a slice of cheese from the lone food tray on the counter, but decide against it.

"Dad, I..."

He doesn't look up. Doesn't turn to face me. Doesn't even acknowledge that he's being spoken to. With a hand on my pocket, tracing the outline of the carton with my fingers, I try again.

"I'm sorry."

He takes another sip.

"For everything. All of it."

He nods. The first real response I've gotten from him all day. It's enough. After Mom's funeral, and Grandad's not long after, I don't think he ever expected to have to go through this all again with his brother. It's fine if it's someone else's relative, even if it's your next-door neighbour or your closest friend, but it's different when it's one of your own.

"I've got the tumours," is all he says, and he still won't look at me. "When it's my time, I'd be much obliged if you and Dani would take care of things. Together. I don't want to put Trish through it."

"Yeah." It's all I can say, and it's not enough.

A tear rolls down his cheek, and I pat the cigarette carton absentmindedly.

"Why did you come back?"

"I had to," I whisper, and I'm not sure if he hears me. "I couldn't... I missed you."

He wipes his face with his suit jacket. "Half an hour left," he says before shuffling out of the kitchen.

I'm alone again.

I try to finish the rest of my beer, but I end up pouring it down the sink instead. There's no buzz, no dizziness, and my stomach keeps churning at the thought of what's being done to my uncle right now. By now, he's no more than a slimy, greasy husk that reeks of spoiled meat.

I suddenly remember it will be our town's version of an open casket funeral, like all the others before, and before I realize it, I'm heaving into the sink. It's nothing but liquid, just beer and bile, and it burns my throat and my sinuses. Tears streaming down my face, I cough the rest of it out.

I'm almost cleaned up when the sound of shattered glass brings about an unnatural silence from the next room. I turn on the tap, rinsing away any evidence of weakness before making my way to the living room.

Trish has Mrs. Henry's arm wrapped around her shoulders and a broken beer bottle at her feet. Dani stands close by, her mouth twisted with a mix of worry and embarrassment. The rest of the room forms a circle around Dad and Mr. Grady.

"I'm only saying." And Mr. Grady raises his hands as if to show he means no harm. "You had a hard time with Eileen's funeral, and your second wife isn't from around here. *And* one of your kids missed the last few funerals."

All eyes are on me and my skin is burning.

"If it's too much," he continues, "I would be glad to step in to help with the first-"

"No!" The sharpness in Dad's voice surprises even him.

"But-"

"No. We take care of our own," says Dad with a quavering voice. "He was my brother. I'll be the first. We take care of our own."

"I'll be the second," I say, stepping into the circle, and feeling vulnerable. Naked. I don't know why I volunteered myself. Is it to atone for leaving?

"And you don't need to worry about Trish," says Dani without looking at anyone, but her posture is straight and her stance is firm. "She knew what she was getting into when she came to live here. This may be her first funeral, but she knows what she has to do."

Trish nods, still trembling, although I'm not sure if anyone is looking at her. I still feel too many eyes on me. With so many busybodies in the house, one of them must have heard me vomiting. Plus, my absence from the festivities has not gone unnoticed. If they all think my dad is too weak to bury my uncle properly, they don't expect anything from me.

"We take care of our own," Dad says, and this time there's power in those words. Mr. Grady backs down.

"It's almost five," whispers Trish, but somehow everyone hears her.

I grab a handful of crackers off the food table and I'm the first one out the door. Dani catches up and walks with me in silence. Eventually we fall to the middle of the crowd.

My stomach is not pleased, but I manage to force down all the crackers. And yet, part of me wishes I had grabbed more. I'll be starving by the time this is all done. That is, if I don't lose my nerve at the sight of Uncle Bob.

As the procession passes by the stone wall that marks the unofficial edge of town, Minnie sits on a fallen log, watching us with her yellow-green eyes. She's aware of what's about to happen, no doubt about that. But she won't follow. With a flick of her mangled ears, she turns to look behind us, towards the old chemical plant. The cause of all our troubles and the reason we have to walk almost four miles to the cemetery. It's bad enough we live so close to that place, but it would be worse if we buried our dead in town.

But even the cemetery isn't far enough. I went all the way to the city, two hours away by car, and still couldn't free myself from the shadow of that chemical plant.

I take in a deep breath and let it all out.

"I was scared," I say to Dani, and she actually looks at me. With the sun low in the sky, I catch the suggestion of her eyes from behind her glasses.

"We're all scared," she says.

"No, I mean... well, yes. But I was scared... out there. In the city. I couldn't do it. It felt safer to come back to the familiar. And I thought... I just got so jumpy. Everything was a tumour waiting to happen. And if something happened to me... if something took root within me before I left home... well, I wanted to be around people who would take care of things, take care of me, the right way. If I'm going to die... that way... I want a proper burial."

She nods, and in that moment, I know that Dad told her about his tumours too. It won't be long before we're planning his funeral.

"I'm glad you came back to us. To me."

"Yeah. Me too. No one understands what we go through. How can they? They don't live it, they don't... they live far away from chemical plants and they have the luxury of being able to burn their dead without worrying about the fumes. But if something happens, if they don't properly handle the corpse, then..." I swallowed hard, picturing the worst-case scenario.

"Someone could get hurt," Dani finishes for me.

"Right. It's... it's better if we stick together. I trust you. I trust you to... well, if go first."

She smirks. "Now, don't start going all soft on me."

"I promise I won't."

I allow myself to smile, but my face hardens and I steel my nerves when the cemetery comes into view. The undertaker is waiting for us between the granite headstones. His young assistant is pale faced with a familiar emptiness in his eyes. This must have been his first one. His first of many vivisections.

We can hear what used to be Uncle Bob before we see him. After almost a decade of funerals, I'm still not used to the sound of their screams.

Supposedly, this is the most humane way of dealing with things, and it gives families the illusion of control in an uncontrollable situation. Yet Dad starts crying when he hears his brother's slurred howling.

"Oh, Bobby," he moans.

The grave is shallow, only three feet deep, because of the bed of limestone beneath the earth. Something about it helps the bodies decay faster. There's some sort of reaction involved, I guess. I never understood it fully, and I don't want to. This isn't a place I like to think too much about. Basically, the unnatural chemical composition of Uncle Bob's body means that he won't last long in this place. And that's a good thing if we botch the funeral. But since the whole community gets involved these days, the risk of "walkers" has decreased over the years.

I step up beside Dad and put my hand on his shoulder as I stare down into the pit. There's no coffin, only what remains of my uncle. Bob's head is rolling around on his flayed body. Receding gums make it appear as if his teeth have grown in death, and his eyes are cloudy. His organs are gone and he's foaming at the mouth. Like a roast that's been picked clean. Patches of flesh are missing from where tumours were removed.

The undertaker has them. He has everything that's no longer inside of my undead uncle.

Undertakers used to remove the brain, thinking that's where they would find answers. That's what all the movies seemed to suggest. They were wrong. Now, the brain is left intact for the benefit of the family. That way, we get to have this grotesque final goodbye. It gives closure. The community is only there to help, to offer support, and to deliver the necessary blown to the brain if one of us is unable or unwilling.

The rest of the organs are all in jars back at the funeral parlor. The few scientists in this town will study them, picking them apart and smearing them across microscope slides, in the hopes they will find a cure. If they can cure the tumours, maybe then they can find a way to make sure the dead stay dead. It's likely they won't. They've been at this for decades, ever since the first chemical spill, and I don't expect the answers will reveal themselves before Dani and I are forced to plan Dad's funeral.

"When you're ready," the undertaker says in a gravelly voice as he hands Dad a metal pole. They treat it like some sort of ceremonial staff, but it's the same as all the others like it at the hardware store.

With a glance over my shoulder, I see the line has already formed. Dani and Trish are waiting behind us. Uncle Bob is our family, so it's up to us to take care of him. Everyone else is here for ceremonial purposes. And for practice when it comes time to do the same to their relatives.

"Bye, Bobby. You were a sonofabitch, but you were my brother. And I loved you."

With a howl, Dad drives the pole into the grave, and the pointed end lands just to the left of Uncle Bob's nose. A solid hit, but not enough to put Bob out of his misery. His head writhes around the pole, and he spits out more foam when it's removed. Wiping the tears from his eyes with the sleeve of his jacket, Dad hands the weapon to me.

He doesn't walk away like I expect him to. No matter how hard this is for him, he knows he needs to see this through till the end.

With a gulp, I reach into my pocket and squeeze the carton of cigarettes. I stare down into Uncle Bob's empty, cavernous torso. I study Dad's fate in amongst the broken ribs and shredded tissue. There's a stray tumour where Bob's lungs should be. A pulsating mass of red that oozes yellow-green puss.

They left his eyes in his skull because Dad didn't consent to have them removed and studied. I wish he had. But I stare into those milky green eyes all the same. I take a deep breath, toss the crumpled pack of cigarettes into the grave and spear my uncle through his right eye before his toxin riddled brain can register what's happened.

His head lolls to the side when I remove the pole. The tip of the mangled cigarette is poking out of the carton from the depths of Bob's chest. The tumour drips on it. There's just enough life, or whatever it is, left in Uncle Bob for Dani.

"You got out for good," I whisper to him like I'm jealous, and an odd suggestion of a smile appears on his lips. But maybe I'm dizzy from the vomiting, and the beer, and the lack of food.

By the time Dani and Trish finish their turn, it's time for the rest of the community to step in, one by one. Not that there's anything left of Uncle Bob's "life force" at this point. Nothing but a gurgle as the cloudy foam dribbles from his lips. Dad puts an arm around Trish's shoulders and wordlessly congratulates her on a job well done. Her first funeral and she didn't faint, vomit, or embarrass the family. Better than my first, that's for sure.

Dani steps a little closer towards me as we witness the town ceremonially murder my uncle. Barely moving, she slips something heavy into my pocket. I pat down on it and it's a small mason jar, I think. When no one is looking, I sneak a peek.

Gherkins. Granddad's favourite. I'm glad Trish got the good kind of pickles, and grateful Dani smuggled them to me. I'll need something to eat when this is all over.

Acknowledgements

Wow, here we are. My fourth short story collection. I had planned on only doing three before moving on to other projects, but this one snuck up on me and demanded publication. And, as my friend / neighbour / beta reader / writing buddy / podcast co-host Trevor says, I am the short story authority. They keep coming, wave after wave. I always thought I'd start off by publishing novels, but the short stories have me firmly in their grasp and there's no escape.

So obviously, I'm going to start out by thanking Trevor. Even though he didn't directly have a hand in these stories, he always pushes me to do better. His mere existence is motivation enough on some days. The second thank you goes to my husband, Mark who also pushes me to succeed. He'll be the first to push me past my comfort zone if he catches even a whiff of stagnation.

Thank you to my inspiration for these stories! I (literally) could not have written these tales of zombies and the undead without you. Thank you to my family members whose doppelgängers inhabit these pages, and thank you to AutoCrit for supplying the writing prompts that spawned some of these dark and gruesome tales.

But writing the stories is only half the work. Thank you to the various people who had a hand in editing the stories in this collection: Jasmine Gower, Katherine D. Graham, Lauren Humphries-Brooks, Daniel Kaplan, and Gloria (my secret weapon). And a huge thank you to James from GoOnWrite.com for another stellar cover. As he was the one who designed the cover for "Cold Cuts & Cigarettes", one of the stories featured in this collection, it just felt right to by another pre-made cover from him.

I don't think I'm forgetting anyone, but if I am I'm sure they'll let me know.

And last but not least, thank you to my wonderful readers. Thank you to those of you who have been following my writing journey from the start and bought a copy of this book right away. And thank to anyone new here who met me at a craft market and decided to give my stories a try. I may say that I can't do what I do without all of the people who help me to publish, but it's really all of you who make this possible.

I hope this zombie apocalypse is to your liking.

Index

my mind turned into the tenants from hell. I actually feel sorry for Ned.

9. Marker: Written for the AutoCrit 2023 Destination Unknown Challenge. We had to start the story with "A name is usually the first thing we learn about a person" and end the story with "Guess you could say I've finally clawed my way to the top." In between, we received the twist: no initial pronouns as sentence starters. That was rough for me since I wrote the story in first person. I made significant changes to the final draft because I did not like the ending we were asked to use. At least, I didn't like the way I had worked it into the story and it didn't feel like something Margaret would ever say.

10. You Want One? I'll Give You Five!: Initially, I wasn't sure about having two list-style stories in this collection, but I loved them both too much. Whereas "Rules for Not Dying" is humorous, I wanted this one to be at the opposite end of the spectrum.

11. Kacie: First "published" as a freebie for anyone who signs up for my newsletter. I've been toying with the idea of writing a new freebie story for some time, and "Kacie" was a good fit for this collection, so it's time to make the change. Keep an eye out for a new freebie in 2024, and sign up to my newsletter to get it!

12. Cold Cuts & Cigarettes: First published as a stand-alone short story. I suppose I could have waited until I found a collection to put it in, but the story is so important to me for many different reasons, so I had to publish it as soon as possible.

Don't miss out!

Visit the website below and you can sign up to receive emails whenever Stephanie Anne publishes a new book. There's no charge and no obligation.

https://books2read.com/r/B-A-IKLN-VFVPC

BOOKS 2 READ

Connecting independent readers to independent writers.

Also by Stephanie Anne

Watch for more at www.stephanieanneauthor.ca.

About the Author

Hello, dear readers. Thank you for stopping by. My name is Stephanie Anne and I am an oddball extraordinaire. My writing assistants include my cats Minerva, Finn, and Bubs. Unfortunately, they like to sleep on the job. I have a love for all things strange and monstrous and I hope you do to. If you like disturbing horror stories and unsettling tales of science-fiction, you've come to the right place. Do stay in touch.

Read more at www.stephanieanneauthor.ca.